CW00406254

Merry Fuckin'

And Other Yuletide Shit

by

Kevin J. Kennedy

Merry Fuckin' Christmas and Other Yuletide Shit
© 2020 Kevin J. Kennedy

Cover design by Michael Bray

First Printing, 2020

Other Books by KJK Publishing

Anthologies

Collected Christmas Horror Shorts

Collected Easter Horror Shorts

Collected Halloween Horror Shorts

Collected Christmas Horror Shorts 2

The Horror Collection: Gold Edition

The Horror Collection: Black Edition

The Horror Collection: Purple Edition

The Horror Collection: White Edition

The Horror Collection: Silver Edition

The Horror Collection: Emerald Edition

The Horror Collection: Pink Edition

The Horror Collection: Pumpkin Edition

100 Word Horrors

100 Word Horrors: Part 2

100 Word Horrors: Book 3

100 Word Horrors: Book 4

Carnival of Horror

The Best of Indie Horror

Novels, Novellas & Collections

Pandemonium by J.C. Michael

You Only Get One Shot by Kevin J. Kennedy & J.C. Michael

Screechers by Kevin J. Kennedy & Christina Bergling

Dark Thoughts by Kevin J. Kennedy

Vampiro and Other Strange Tales of the Macabre

Acknowledgements

I'd like to thank my prereaders Natasha Sinclair, Ann Keeran & J.C. Michael for all their help. I'd like to thank Michael Bray for another stunning cover. I'd also like to thank everyone who follows me and makes this all possible. Last but not least, I'd like to thank my mum, wife and daughter. 2020 has been the worst year of my life. We lost my father and we have spent a great deal of time together. It's helped and I'm glad we still have each other. I think everyone has had a tough 2020. I hope this book makes you laugh, scream, worry, cringe, or maybe just takes you away from reality for a little while. I wish you all the best in 2021 and let's just hope for a year that is a little easier than this one. Merry Fuckin' Christmas!

Kev

Praise for the book:

"As gritty as Irvine Welsh and as horrific as anything King has put out. Christmas has never been so dark. This is a collection horror fans do not want to miss." **Lee Mountford, Author of The Demonic.**

"Kennedy is one of the modern greats of seasonal horror. Sit by the fireplace, pour yourself a drink and get this read." **Lex H. Jones, author of The Old One and The Sea.**

"Superb! Stylistic! Downright terrifying! Kennedy does not pull any punches." **Christopher Motz, author of Pine Lakes, and Tenants.**

"Freaky, disturbing, unpleasant... These stories could ruin your Christmas!" **Mark Cassell, author of The Shadow Fabric.**

"Everything Kennedy touches turns to gold. And for good reason. A gruesome, rock 'n' roll, festive feast." **Kyle M. Scott, author of The Club.**

Table of Contents

Christmas in Hell

You know, I always hated Christmas. It just wasn't for me. I hated that it had nothing to do with the religious side of it anymore and was basically a retail-run holiday in which everyone felt obligated to spend money they didn't have on shit that they gifted out to people who would never use it. Over the years I received some ridiculous gifts - that I can only assume were recycled from the year before. Some of those gifts must have been in circulation for years now. If you didn't already know, lots of people stockpile the gifts that they get that they consider to be shit, for want of a better word. These items remain in a closet for the next eleven months or so, until the current owner decides to rewrap them in some new paper, add a new little name tag and hey, presto, they spent fuck-all but still have a gift for your ass. Everyone is a winner. Well, except you. You then need to hold onto that piece of shit until next year, until you can palm it off on some other unlucky asshole.

Anyway, I digress. 'Christmas is shit' was always my motto. I did enjoy time I spent with loved ones, but I always enjoyed that at any time of year. I enjoyed eating too much but then again, it's not like I'm exactly strict with my diet throughout the year. The time off work was probably the only bit I really appreciated. I wasn't one of those Grinchlike assholes, though. I didn't spend the season telling others how it was all shit and try to get them to see things my way. People are entitled to do their own thing. Who am I to tell them what to enjoy and what to avoid? At the end of the day, I was roped into spending the same cash as everyone else and playing along, otherwise my wife and daughter would have killed me. Living with two women is never easy, but try disappointing them on a special occasion and just see how difficult your life becomes.

I suppose that brings us onto the point of my story. I'm in Hell. Not the 'my life is falling apart and I'm getting all dramatical about it' kind of hell.... like the actual, real Hell. It's not going to be one of those stories where I tell you that I'm not supposed to be here and then go on a mission to find my way out of Hell. Neither is this story about me defeating some great evil, even though it means I need to stay in Hell forever. It's much less grand than that.

I arrived in October and its now the twenty-fourth of December. Wherever Hell is, they celebrate Christmas here, too. *Of course, they fucking do*, I can almost hear you saying. It's not for the same reasons people on Earth do, and what goes on is very different, but it's called Christmas none the less and it's celebrated on the same date. There is a Santa Claus of sorts and he does leave presents for some. Those are the main similarities. Everything else is a hellish parody of what I once knew and hated.

When I first arrived in Hell, I was sitting in a waiting room. The heating was turned up several times higher than any Earth- bound heating system could have achieved. I imagine the temperatures would have matched that of a furnace and yet there was no fire. The room was being heated by air vents pumping into the reception area. I wasn't sweating; I didn't catch on fire, but the discomfort I felt was insane. There was a desk with a sign above it saying 'Welcome to Hell'. I approached, but as I did the small creature behind the desk held up its paw and abruptly said, "We'll call you, please take a seat," before going back to its newspaper. I moved back to a seat and collapsed into it. My body was in no physical pain, but the incredible heat was debilitating. After two hours of sitting around getting more and more agitated, I approached the desk again. I got an identical response. When I tried to press the matter, I was ignored. The small red creature that had been there before had gone and had been replaced by a slightly larger creature completely covered it blue fur. It reminded me of Cousin Itt from the Addams Family TV show. The creature was reading the same newspaper that the last creature had left behind. I went a little mental for a good few minutes, shouting at the new person behind the desk but when it finally sunk in that the creature hadn't as much as raised its head, no security was coming for me and almost no one seemed to be paying any attention at all, I returned to my seat again.

After somewhere in the neighbourhood of twelve hours, my name was called. I rushed to the desk to be told to go into room six-six-six. Not only was it a cliché... it was the only room. I got into the room and sat in front of me was one of the most gorgeous women I have ever seen—apart from the two extra arms she was sporting—she was a perfect ten.

"Please take a seat," she told me.

I took a seat.

"Can you tell me why I'm here?" I asked her.

"You're here for your work assignment," came her reply.

"No, I mean why am I in Hell? Wait… what? My work assignment?" I asked, confused.

"Yes, your work assignment."

The conversation went nowhere fast.

I could take you over the hours and hours that we went round in circles but it would put you to sleep. What I can tell you, is that I learned a few things. Firstly, no one in Hell is going to answer any of your questions. People will often give you pieces of information in general conversation, but never as an answer to a question that you asked. Secondly, time in Hell runs the same as it does on Earth, or at least it feels that way. What I didn't realise until a bit later is that when you aren't progressing with whatever is expected of you in Hell, time just stops completely and waits for you. It moves on when you do. The best example I can give you of this started occurring in noticeable scales when I began my first job.

My first job began directly after the meeting that I spent hours in trying to find out why I had a work assignment in the first place. When I left the little interview room, feeling pretty exasperated, I walked into a much larger room that held a mixture of people and creatures of various assortments that must have been in the thousands. Each sat in front of PC's with headsets on chattering away. A soppy-looking blonde girl with a grin too large, appeared next to me wearing a oversized t-shirt that read, 'welcome to the call centre'. *Typical,* I thought to myself. What else would be my given profession in Hell but a damn Telesales Advisor? I should have known. It turned out that for eight to twelve hours a day, I would be on the phones, cold calling people to try and sell them crap that they didn't need. The extra catch in Hell was that no one ever got a sale. Ever! I tried hanging up on customers that the system had called and put through to my line, hanging onto the call after the customer had hung up and various different techniques that were applied regularly in the call centre industry when you just couldn't be bothered. None of them worked. As I said earlier, if you weren't doing what you were supposed to be doing, time just stopped for you. It didn't seem to affect those around you, so I'm not quite sure of the logistics of it, but, still... time stopped all the same. Now everything was kind of irrelevant since it wasn't like anyone had anything better to do than to work at telesales all day, every day, with no chance of ever having a buying customer; 'tis tough on the mind. Oh, and we don't get weekends off. It's a seven-day-week. We do get paid, though, and while it's Hell, there's no one here whipping and torturing us. As crazy as it sounds, some days I think I'd swap a day in the call centre for a savage whipping.

When I got off work from my first shift I was given a token for twenty hell notes. It was a fifth of my day's salary. Everyone was paid daily in Hell. You got a fifth of your salary and the rest went straight into your Christmas account. The money could only be lifted the week before Christmas and could only be spent on Christmas gifts. You couldn't even buy yourself one. We walked through a doorway that looked like it took you into another room, instead, it led into a park, I ranted loudly that this seemed like bullshit to me. I was informed that there was simply no way around it. The various call centre workers headed in every direction. I wasn't sure where any of the directions took you, so I just stood there looking dumb. After deciding it didn't really matter where I went, I just started walking in a straight line. I came to an edge of the park that was completely surrounded by a twenty- foot- high fence, dripping in barbed wire. There were three doorways with signs above them. They read, 'Halloweenland', 'The Gate' and 'Just Relax'. Obviously, I picked the one marked 'Just Relax' and quickly left the park.

To say it was a mistake would be an understatement. I spent the next fifteen or so hours being tortured before being released to go to work in the morning. I'm sure I died a few times, but each time something serious happened to my body it seemed like I blacked out and would wake up okay again... only for the torture to start all over. I was let go fifteen minutes before my shift began. I decided not to go into work and sat in the park for hours. After wandering around the perimeter of the park a few times and realising every door in the gate had disappeared, apart from the call centre one, I gave in and went to work. I thought maybe I would meet someone that could help me out a little. I was wrong. When I arrived, the shift was just beginning. Time had waited for me. I spent another day calling customers who wouldn't buy anything before leaving into the park again. I repeated this routine daily, every day finding new doors to try but each was as bad, if not worse, than the last. I thought a few times about just staying in the park, yet my mind kept niggling at me, whispering that one never knew if there might exist a good door to be found. When no one will answer any questions, it's difficult what to know about anything.

The weeks went by and I made no progress in discovering anything other than small quirks to Hell; nothing of any real use. They start celebrating Christmas in early November. That's one of the things that was hard to miss. I think it was around the tenth of November when I walked out the usual door at the end of my shift to find the park covered in fake snow with a massive Christmas tree in the middle. It was no different from Christmas trees on Earth in the way it was decorated. The only small difference was it leaked blood instead of sap. Although the actual day was a long way off and the money wasn't released for a while, it became apparent it was just another method of torture. Christmas songs played twenty- four hours a day or rather longer if time stopped for you for any reason. They played through the call centre headsets between calls, from speakers that were positioned everywhere, inside and out, and from the random places that the mystery doors took you to between shifts. Some of the songs I had liked in the beginning, others I'd always hated and some I'm sure had been made up badly on purpose just as an extra measure of pain. Not only did we have to listen to the shit non-stop, but we had to actually sing carols on breaks. The entire call centre had to stand at their desks and sing carols at the top of their voices for both fifteen minute breaks and their lunch as well. Not that any of them had to eat and no one went to the toilet in Hell, but it seemed to make the day even longer. I tried again to just not do it and my fifteen minute break went on and on. I gave up in the end and sung along. Miraculously, in Hell, you will know the words to every single carol in existence, even if you didn't before.

As time passed, I realised that no one made friends in Hell, it was part of the plan. No one tried, although I'm sure everyone wanted to. I couldn't work out if the ones who seemed to have a little more control in the call centre were born in Hell or had been here longer. What granted them the privileged role of being able to wander about and occasionally talk to each other, but, really, who knows if they are actual conversations or just another strange going-on of Hell? Our call scripts that we had to stick to, word- for-word on every call without deviation, suddenly changed. We were calling customers to sell them Christmas products at massively reduced prices. No one bought anything. I wondered if we were calling real people or if it was some kind of simulation that had us believing we were talking to someone. I seemed capable of independent thought. It was everything else that I had no control over.

It was almost like I was watching a movie of myself having a shitty life but couldn't exert any control over the situation.

The weeks continued to pass and it reached the week before Christmas. The eighty percent of our salary that had been kept back was released to us in the form of a card with a Christmas parcel on the front. When I found the gates at the edge of the park on that night, each just said 'Presents' above it. I picked the middle gate for no reason other than I was standing in front of it. It took me to the largest department store I had ever seen. It was the stuff of nightmares. Now some of you may think that sounds like a pretty fun evening, you're wrong. Shopping is an evil pursuit. You are surrounded with morons who pay no attention to where they are going, bump into you then look at you as if it's your fault. The stores are always too hot, but, to be fair, pretty much everywhere is too hot in Hell. There are people looking for money from you for one thing or another on every corner. The queues are ridiculous, and stale alcohol reeks from those around you. I can't lie... I've never seen the attraction to being surrounded by a large crowd, and shopping often put me in a place where I hated everyone and everything. Now, that was my experience on Earth—in Hell it's so much worse. The shopping centre only plays the one Christmas song on repeat endlessly, so there is that to deal with. We all get a tour guide because the centre is so large. I got my ex-girlfriend. To say that she was an absolute bawbag on Earth would be an understatement, but, in Hell, she talks even more shit. None of what she says makes sense, not that it really ever did. She bursts into tears every twenty minutes or so and irrationally tells me how it's my fault—again, talking mainly gibberish that I'm not sure anyone would understand—and worst of all I couldn't lose her. Every time I tried, I turned around and she was standing next to me.

Each day I'd try a different door in the park and every time I would be back in the same shopping centre with the same ex doing the same shit. This lasted until the day before Christmas, today. The day at work was the same as always. There was no party or games or anything else… just another shift of meaningless labour. As I walked out into the park, I thought something festive might be going on, but other than the tree and lights, it was the same. Everyone made their way to various gates on different sides of the park. I sat around for a while, wondering if I would have to spend the day with my ex again. I reasoned that surely Christmas Eve wouldn't be more shopping. When I got to the doors they read 'Griswold', 'Kingston Falls', and 'Hill Valley'. I had no idea what any of them meant, so I went into 'Hill Valley', thinking that it at least sounded like a nice place. It didn't so much take me anywhere as much as transport me into the future.

I found myself, on Christmas day, at a dinner with the Devil. The real one: big guy, red all over, horns, disproportionately large upper body with small legs. Yep, that's right, dinner with the Devil. Just him and me. I did wonder if somehow everyone had dinner with the Devil on Christmas day. Time was strange and I'm sure he could have arranged it had he wanted to. I didn't imagine I was special. What I did find a little disconcerting was the Santa Claus costume he wore. It wasn't evil and terrifying, just the normal costume that Santa wore on Earth and it looked high- end. I can't imagine the Devil has money problems.

I just sat there looking at him. I wasn't sure what to say. We sat at either end of a long table. No one else was in the lavishly decorated room. After staring at him for a minute, wondering if I should say something, I realised this was the first time since I came to Hell that I wasn't being roasted. The room temperature was actually comfortable. It would appear that the Devil doesn't like it toasty.

Moments later a large set of doors opened and in came a troop of what looked to be female elves, apart from the fact that they were bright red like the Devil. Each was naked, wearing only sets of multi coloured Christmas lights. They carried trays of food which they placed along the table before disappearing back through the door. The Devil noticed me looking over everything.

"You can eat today, son."

My eyes quickly moved to him. "I thought no one ate in Hell."

"Well, you can eat today."

It wasn't exactly the in depth sort of answer I was looking for but I was getting used to knowing next to nothing in this new life. I grabbed what looked to be a turkey leg and devoured it in a few bites, the juice dripping from my chin.

"Help yourself, boy, for tomorrow you go back to the start."

"What do you mean I go back to the start?" I asked.

"Back to the day you came here. You start all over again," he answered. He didn't eat. He just sat smiling and watching me.

"What the fuck? I need to go through all this shit again? What's even the point to it?" I bellowed, standing up and slamming my fists on the table. Fuck the Devil, right?

I did kind of regret it as soon as I had done it. I was waiting for him to spring across the table and rip my throat out, but he didn't—he didn't even move. He just waited for me to take my seat again. It was all a bit embarrassing if I'm being honest.

"Feel better?" he asked with a knowing smirk.

"A little," I answered honestly. It's always good to blow off a bit of steam, even if you do feel like a fool afterwards.

"Good. Now. I have a proposal for you."

"A proposal? Don't you control everything here?" I blinked in genuine surprise.

"No one controls everything anywhere, son. I'm looking for a replacement demon. One of my seasonal demons was killed and I need to get a replacement for next year. I gave my son a shot at it this year after he wouldn't stop hounding me about it, but he will make a mess of it like he does everything else. The lad is truly evil, but if I said he had shit for brains, I'd be insulting the shit. Anyway... the job. I need a new Krampus. You know who that is, right?"

I did, at this point, wonder if I was having the longest, weirdest dream of my entire life, but it was all too real. The smells and the details weren't dreamlike at all.

"You want me to be Krampus? The anti-Santa. Big blue guy that looks a bit like you and hates Christmas? Are you serious? Why the fuck would I want to do that?"

The whole set up in Hell is weird as shit, but this was next level crazy.

"I've watched you. You've kept more of your own mind and memories than any of the others. I'm tired of replacing my minions constantly. You know, the saying that you can't get good staff is so true. I'm surrounded by idiots everywhere I go."

I had to remind myself that the Devil wasn't having a heart-to-heart with me. I wondered if he'd had one too many drinks before dinner.

"Why would I want to be one of your minions? No offence, but we aren't exactly well acquainted. Your back story precedes you and by all accounts, they say that you're a bit of an asshole. On top of all that, this place is insane. You're in charge. What about that says 'good boss' material?"

The Devil actually threw his head back and burst into a fit of laughter.

"Son, the way I see it, you can keep going back to the day you arrived and live through our extended Christmas season for eternity or, you can go through the transformation and return to Earth where you will hunt and kill throughout the Christmas season, year after year. Now tell me, which of those two ideas sounds like the most fun?"

I've got to be honest. The moral side of me was screaming at me to tell him where he could shove his job, that I could never take it, but if I'm truly honest with you, I just really hate Christmas.

As I said at the start, there is no great epiphany. I'm not going to spend eternity trying to redeem myself. In actual fact, I'm not all that sure what I did wrong to end up here in the first place. Either way, here I am, back on Earth, leaving my story for someone to find. It may become a new legend that parents tell their children and then pass into myth as time goes on or, maybe no one will ever read it. Who knows? I will tell you one thing, though. The next time I hear a Christmas carol, I'm going to tear everyone in the room to pieces. Merry Krampus.

The End

Sisterly Love

I bought her a sexy little Mrs Claus outfit from the lingerie store. I thought she'd love it.

"Who would wear something like this?" she asked, holding it out and looking at me as if I was stupid.

Your sister for one, I thought to myself, picturing the evening before when I fucked her sister in the matching costume I'd bought her.

In the end I just left. I could never bring myself to knock her off. We had been in love.

Her sister wouldn't have it though.

"I'll kill the bitch myself" she said, storming out into the snow.

The End

Merry Fuckin' Christmas

Christmas Eve is a time for joy, a time to celebrate, to relax with your family, to drink and be merry. It's a time of year when very few people walk the streets, snow falls from the sky and the drab greys are lost to the beauty of a glistening white landscape.   Re-runs of old movies take over the television, Christmas songs filter out from every store you pass, colourful lights sparkle in the windows of every house. It's a time to forget about life's troubles if only for a day and look forward to the Christmas dinner.

Christmas dinner was Alec's favourite dinner of the year. He got up first thing in the morning, often before even the kids were awake, to start preparing. The turkey was covered in bacon, and apples were sliced and placed around it for flavour, the stock later being used to make a mouth-watering gravy. He would cut the vegetables and place them into separate bowls to cook later. Next he would set the table. Christmas was the one and only day of the year they used a tablecloth. It was white with little bits of red and green trim. Pauline, Alec's wife had bought the tablecloth a few years ago and they had used it every year since. It looked nice adorned with the silverware that they also only used for Christmas. The family wasn't religious, but Christmas wasn't really a religious holiday anymore.

The retail chains owned Christmas now. The 1st of October this year, the stores filled with Christmas decorations, the same day they put out the Halloween decorations. It made no sense, and Alec felt it ruined it all a bit, but at least by Christmas Eve he was home with his family, and he could shut out all the world's problems, if only for twenty-four hours.

Alec finished setting the table by placing a few Christmas crackers between the plates. He could smell the turkey cooking, the smell wafting in from the kitchen. It made his mouth water. He always cooked little sausages in with the turkey and by the time it was ready, they fell apart in your mouth. They were his favourite part; the kids loved them too. Christmas had been all about the kids the last few years: seeing their little faces light up with joy as they tore the paper from their presents, only to fling them aside and grab the next one. They were spoiled, Alec knew, but he just couldn't help himself, he would have spent his last penny on them just to see they were happy.

Walking into the kitchen, Alec opened the oven, then stepped back as the heat spilled out, he grabbed a fork from the shelf and speared three of the little sausages. He closed the oven door then began carefully nibbling on the piping hot sausages stacked on his fork. He leaned against the kitchen unit, staring into space as he finished them off, then threw the fork in the sink. The house was eerily quiet, something Alec wasn't used to. You didn't get a lot of quiet time with a wife and two kids. Sarah, who was the older of the two, was reasonably manageable, but his five year old son, Sammy, was a lunatic. The boy only seemed to need occasional small naps, then wake up with a whirlwind of energy. He could tire out both Alec and Pauline in a matter of an hour, however, he was a good boy overall, just noisy and energetic. Alec walked over to the unit on the wall just to the side of the kitchen window, opened it and slipped out a bottle of whisky. He took his glass from beside the sink and filled it with three fingers then knocked it back in one shot. The burn going down his throat felt good. '*Daddy*' he heard, but only in his head: there would be no one shouting at him as they came running down the stairs, sounding like a heard of wild elephants, no wife to kiss his cheek and wish him a Merry Christmas, no one to sit at the table with and share his meal, no one to look at and feel filled with love just because they are part of his life. No...fucking...one!

Alec launched the glass across the kitchen, smashing it into a million tiny fragments. He picked up the bottle and upended it, taking several gulps before thumping it back down onto the work top. His throat was on fire but it felt good. It felt like the anger that was buzzing around in his head was somewhere else, if only momentarily. Alec knew he would never have a good Christmas ever again. His family had been taken from him, stolen by a scummy, drunk driver that had walked free, all because the law was a fucking joke. His lawyer had told him in layman's terms that the police had fucked up, it was that simple. His family was gone and the guy got off. No justice, no retribution, just a big 'fuck you!' Alec lifted the bottle and took another drink of the whisky; it was having little effect. He had been drinking pretty heavily for weeks now, and it was taking more and more to have any effect. No matter how much Alec tried to move on, he knew he couldn't; there was nothing to move on to. His wife and his children had been his life, his sole purpose for living; without them, he was nothing and had no reason to go on living. For him, Christmas wasn't a time for joy, for family, for forgetting about life's miseries. Instead, It was a time for giving up, self-loathing, pity, anger, hatred, and...revenge! Alec knew what he had to do, knew what this Christmas Eve was for. It was God's gift to him. The God that no one feared or celebrated anymore and had been replaced by Santa Claus. Alec thought about Christmas and all its modern traditions and smiled to himself. It had all been fun and games while he had a family but now that they were gone he could see how stupid it all was. It was just another distraction, given to the masses so they could be led like sheep through a life of pain by the few who held the power that those same masses gave them. People were weak and no longer fought for anything they believed; it was easier to go home and watch the TV and forget about it all. Not any fucking more, Alec thought to himself. *Tonight there will be consequences*, he thought, leaving the kitchen with the bottle still in hand.

***

The snow was falling heavily, there was already a good eight or nine inches on the ground. It was cold out but Alec felt nothing. The side of the drunk driver's house was pretty secluded by the high wooden fence, so that the only way he would be seen is if someone was walking by the front of the house and looked down, which was unlikely on a night like this. Alec didn't really give a fuck but, he didn't want to get arrested before he got started; just like Santa Claus he had more than one person to visit tonight. Alec had half-expected to find the drunk driver sitting alone, in a pile of his own filth, feeling miserable. It was just the impression he had of drunk drivers but, looking through the small side window he could see that, in fact, the man had a family just like the one Alec used to have. Two kids, and a wife! Un-fucking-believable! It was too bad the family was here to witness what Alec had planned, but his mind was made up. Alec was left without a family, and now the driver's family would be left without a father/husband. *It's not a time of year for giving*, he thought, *it's a time of year for taking away.*

The snow crunched quietly underfoot as Alec made his way around the back of the house. It was a nice neighbourhood, so Alec could only hope that the family didn't lock their doors. He couldn't believe the man who took his family lived on a nicer street than he could ever afford. He had to wonder if this man was somehow connected to someone in power, having seemingly gotten off so easily. Alec reached out and tried the handle and the door popped open. The houses in the street were pretty new and the door opened silently. Although he didn't want to alert the family to his arrival, he wasn't exactly going for a stealth job here. He would enter, take the man and leave. He walked through the kitchen and stopped behind the door, because he knew when he opened it he would be in the dining room where the family was sitting.

"Is it getting cold in here?" he heard come from through the door. He turned to see he had left the kitchen door open and the cold night air was spilling in. *Fuck it*, he thought to himself before pushing the door open and bursting in. Screams filled the air instantly. One of the little girls jumped up from her chair and ran to her mother's side. Alec pulled the large kitchen knife from the inside of his jacket.

"You! Cunt! Come with me or they all die. I'm not here to fuck about, I'm not here to argue with you or make a deal. You get up out of your chair and come with me if you want your family to live. You know who I am. You stood watching me in court, looking smug while getting your 'not guilty' verdict. Well you are guilty, and you will pay but your family doesn't have to." Alec said, pointing the knife straight at the driver.

"Okay, okay. Don't hurt them. I'll come." The driver replied.

"Barry!" the woman screamed, hugging the girl tight to her side and reaching over the table to grab his arm.

"It's okay, honey. I'm just going to go with the man and sort this out." Barry replied.

"Move!" Alec demanded.

Barry got up from his chair and slowly moved around the side of the table that was empty. He never took his eyes from Alec. Alec knew that most men would do whatever it took to protect their family, so he had counted on the driver coming quietly. Alec kept the knife pointed at him as he passed into the kitchen then followed him out without looking back at the family. Scaring the two girls was a sad, unintentional consequence of today's events, and Alec knew they would always remember the bad man who took their father away. But really, what choice did he have when it was their father that caused all of this? And Alec would see to it... Barry had to pay!

***

Four hours later

Alec pulled his jeep into his driveway, groans coming from the backseat as he did. The snow was still coming down heavily, which had been a godsend in keeping his actions discreet throughout the evening. The roads were empty and no one was walking anywhere at this late hour. It was almost approaching midnight. The kiddies would be wrapped up in their beds to allow Santa to do his rounds and the parents would be trying to squeeze in some much needed rest before the big day. Alec turned and looked over the seat at the Chief of Police, tied up and gagged in the back of his car.

"Now we are going to go inside. I'm sure all my neighbours will be asleep and as you know it's a very important time of year. I would appreciate very much if you could keep the noise down as we go in. I could always just knock you out so you can't make a noise but I am affording you the opportunity to behave yourself. The downside being that if you don't behave things will be much worse for you. Do you understand?"

The Chief of Police nodded his head, sweat was running down his brow. It was clear he had been struggling but Alec knew he was going nowhere. Alec came round the side of the jeep and opened the door before pulling the Chief out into the snow. Not bothering to lift him into a standing position he dragged him through the snow to his door, leaving a furrow behind them. He took his keys out quietly and unlocked the door. Taking one last look around his street and seeing it was deserted he dragged the Chief inside. Last year when he stood outside the front door having a smoke before he went to bed, he had never felt so good. Tonight though, the only positive feeling was that he had achieved what he had set out to do. The night, however, was far from over.

***

Sweat dripped from Alec's head in the kitchen. It had taken him the last few hours to get everything prepared. The turkey had only needed warming up but he had to cook the vegetables and make the gravy. His kitchen was pretty small so the heat built up quickly. He removed the turkey from the cooking tray and settled it on the platter. Lifting it with care he walked back through into the living room and gently placed it in the middle of the still decorated table.

"Get anyone a drink?" he asked, looking around at his guests, before chuckling to himself.

The three men were tied securely to the hard backed dining chairs, their mouths tightly gagged. They looked from Alec to each other, their eyes filled with fear. Alec felt that people should pay for their transgressions on this most holy of evenings, and especially those he deemed responsible for the tragic loss of his family. Alec had spent the evening rounding them up. They were: the driver who had killed his family, the chief of the police station where the evidence was conveniently lost, and the local politician, primarily because he was a useless, corrupt fuck. Alec left and went back to the kitchen.

Twenty minutes later Alec had laid out all the food, the room smelled gorgeous. For a split second, as Alec left the kitchen for the last time that night, he saw his family sitting around the table, only for the briefest instant and then he was back with the three men--the three wrong doers who represented the problem with this world and the reason that Alec felt like he had no reason left to play the game of being a good guy anymore. His entire life he had questioned himself about the way things worked and often found that though he disagreed with the world on a basic moral level, it was never quite enough to do anything about it at the time. Now everything was different and he no longer felt the need to conform to society and it's ridiculous rules. The people in charge weren't looking out for his best interests so he would do it himself in any way he saw fit, and this was the start.

"Now gentleman, I know what you're all thinking. Yes, the food does smell delicious, and no, you wont be able to eat with the gags in your mouths. It's not for you. I just wanted to do this one last time." As he finished speaking, a single tear ran down Alec's cheek. "I loved my family you know, truly loved them. I suppose most people say that, but I really did. You don't know what you have until it's gone." As Alec stopped speaking again, instead of sinking into thoughtfulness, this time his face hardened and his brow furrowed. "But you! You cunts took everything from me! Every fucking thing! Look around this place. Does it look like a fucking bachelor pad?" he asked rhetorically. "No!" he answered himself and continued, "It fuckin' doesn't! Do you know why? Because it was a family home, FAMILY! Do you know what I'm saying? A family home." Alec knew he was getting too worked up and didn't want any of his neighbours calling the cops before he was finished.

"I'm sorry gentlemen, my emotions got the better of me. One moment please." Alec got up and went back to the kitchen, returning with a new bottle of whisky.

"I'd offer you a drink but…..well, you know." He snickered.

The three men could barely budge since their restraints were so tight. Their eyes flickered nervously from each other to Alec, knowing that the situation couldn't be much worse. The driver, Barry, knew his wife would have called the cops by now. The police chief lived alone, and, since having anyone else around was often someone who ended up knowing too much, so did the politician.

"Now. I've been drinking a lot, gents, and while this all seems to have gone rather smoothly, I didn't actually think it through a whole lot. You see, I want you all dead and while I am sure you all would strongly disagree, I truly believe the world will be a better place without the likes of you three." All three of the men were grunting through the gags now, obviously trying to explain their own reasons for past transgressions.

"I'm sorry guys. It's not an 'explain yourself and walk out of here' kind of night. You will all die at this very table. This will be the last Christmas dinner that any of us have—not that you will be eating much." Alec suddenly broke out in a crazy grin. "You have to admit I put on a great spread for you." The crazy grin disappeared as suddenly as it had appeared, and Alec grew somber once again as he continued, "My wife always used to say I loved Christmas more than the kids did; maybe she was right."

Leaning over the table Alec used the long, thin lighter to light the candles before getting up and dimming the lights. The snow continued falling outside as Alec started to speak again. "My wife liked to eat by candlelight, We probably didn't do it enough now that I think about it. I have a lot of regrets, if I'm honest. You always think there will be more time, but there wasn't… WAS THERE!?" Alex roared, standing up and flipping the table over, all the food flying everywhere. The turkey smashed against the wall and the three men and most of the living room were covered in vegetables. The gravy landed on the politicians lap, burning him, causing the man to reflexively kick his chair over, landing him on his back. Alec stormed out of the room and returned with a claw hammer. He walked over to the bottle of whisky that lay on its side on the floor, spilling out some of its contents and picked it up. He took a large drink and, still clutching the bottle, dropped his arm back to his side. The men looked terrified, they both had their eyes glued to him while the politician stared at the ceiling. Alec sat the bottle in the middle of the floor and hoisted the politician back into an upright position, telling the man sarcastically. "Wouldn't want you to miss any of the fun now, would we?"

As Alec made his way over to his laptop, he smiled to himself as he heard at least one of the men crying; his wife had cried as she died in his arms, their two small children dead already in the backseat. The car had flipped several times after the collision, but landed upright. Alec had been the only one to survive; he wished he hadn't. After the laptop was fired up, he clicked into his Christmas music and played 'Santa Claus, You Cunt' by Kevin Bloody Wilson. He had always liked this one because it made him laugh, though his wife had warned him the kids had better not hear it. For this reason, he'd waited until the children were in bed before he'd played it.

'Santa Claus, you cunt! Where's me fuckin bike, I've opened all this other sh…..' drifted out from the speakers as Alec approached the men. "Okay gentlemen. I think we have wasted quite enough time." Then like lightening he swung the hammer above his head and brought it back down, blunt-side first, right into the politician's forehead. Before the man's head had even bounced back he let out a torrent of blows all over it. He quickly flipped the hammer over and brought the claw side down, sinking it right through the top of the politician's skull. When he let go of the hammer, it stayed in place. Blood started to run down the length of the handle and drip onto the carpet as the room filled with the scent of piss and shit. He looked at the mess of the skull. For the first time he realised the other two men were screaming through their gags; everything had gone silent while he worked. He realised he didn't even hear the music that had been playing. He admired his work for another few seconds and returned to the laptop to restart the song.

Santa Claus, you cunt! Where's me fuckin'…' started to play again. "You know I think as the years pass by, the world becomes a worse place. We move forward with technology and medicine and various other things but none of it's real; we are just mice in a cage. I've decided to get off the wheel now, guys, which means you are both pretty fucked. I'm sure you will now realise I am serious. I want you to think about this question: why shouldn't someone kill a policeman?" he asked staring at the police chief. "Because you spent a few months at police college? Because you are supposed to uphold the law? You are a bunch of corrupt, drug-taking pussies. A force filled with bully-victims turned bully that look the other way when they are needed. A joke!" Alec stopped his rant and walked over to the bottle of whisky, lifted it and took two good swigs, then turned his attention to the other man. "And you!" he roared. "A fucking drunk driver who takes the lives of others because he is too much of a pussy to control his addiction. A man who has a family, though he has no care or consideration for others and their families. No!...I don't accept that either of you have a place on this earth." Alec glanced at the clock. "It's Christmas day you know. I should be getting up in a few hours to start making a lovely dinner for my family but instead I made one for you cunts—the people who took them. Not quite as pleasing I have to say. So! Who's next?!"

Both men started trying to plead through their gags, shaking their heads from side to side and nearly spilling their chairs over onto the floor. 'Silent Night' had clicked onto the laptop and Alec laughed. "It would be a silent night if it wasn't for you two," he said, grinning and looking between the two men. "What?

That's fucking funny!" As he said it he stepped out and to the side and swung the biggest punch he had ever swung in his life. When his arm hit the cop in the side of the head, it felt like he had shattered every bone in his hand. The cop's lights went out and the chair flew onto its side onto the carpet. "Motherfucker!!" Alec raged, rubbing the hand that punched the cop with his other hand. "Ooohhhh, that felt good!" Alec now had a manic look in his eyes. He had drunk well over a bottle of whisky today and for the first time all day, he was starting to feel drunk. "Let's wake him up. I've always heard people calling the cops, pigs or bacon. Let's see shall we?" and with that Alec left for the kitchen. He came back shortly after, still smiling. Barry thought Alec had truly lost it now. Earlier, when Alec broke into Barry's house and kidnapped him, Alec had looked ok at that point. Now he looked deranged, wild-eyed, his eyes constantly flicking from side to side, unable to settle. He marched across the living room and started dragging the unconscious cop across the floor. He yanked him upright before pulling him through the doorway. There were a few seconds of silence, then an ear-splitting scream, followed shortly after by the smell of charred flesh. Barry figured that Alec had pressed the police officer's face to the stove- there was no other explanation for what he was hearing and smelling. The cop's hands were tied by his sides and they hadn't been in the kitchen long enough for Alec to untie him. Barry knew he was going to die here tonight. He thought about his family and hoped they would be okay without him. He had had a drinking problem for a long time, and any mistakes he'd made, his wife did her best to cover for him, and his kids loved him. He couldn't deny that he was guilty for the death of this man's family but he didn't want to die, just like he hadn't wanted to go to prison. Money sorted most things out, but he doubted he could buy his way out of this one. Still, he hoped he would have enough time to try. The screams coming from the other room continued.

Surely the neighbours must have heard that, Barry thought to himself.

Someone must have called the police. As Barry thought about rescue, Alec appeared in the doorway again, dragging the dead cop with him. The man's face was a mess of burnt tissue: bright red and bubbling with ring shapes imprinted on it. A knife was buried in his ear. "Making too much noise, so he was. I got a little carried away, but I can't go waking up the neighbours at this time on Christmas day." The smile was now pasted onto Alec's face; he really did look like he had lost it. He walked across the room, stopped in front of Barry and proceeded to untie the gag from the back of his head. "I don't suppose it matters if you scream now, does it? It's not like you will be any louder than the pig was. Oh, and by the way, he didn't smell like bacon. It's all bullshit." As Alec finished speaking, he remained standing in front of Barry but his mind seemed to wander off. Here was his opportunity, Barry thought.

"Alec, I have money, lots of it. You have seen my house, you know I'm well-off. You've already had your fun. Let me help make the pain go away; money can solve a lot of problems. By tomorrow you could be gone, sitting on a warm beach, sipping a cocktail. Fuck! You could start a new family with the kind of cash I could give you." As Barry finished his sentence he knew he had gone too far. He saw the smile slip from Alec's face.

"Oh! I could start a new family could I? Set me up with a new life, make me happy? Is that what you think you will do? How about this? I'll make you a deal. I'll untie you and let you walk out of here free if you can do one thing for me. Give me my family back—not a new one, the one I had before I crossed paths with you. Can you do that? Can you give me my fucking family back, Barry?!"

Barry didn't know what to say to save his life: no amount of pleading, or begging, or any type of bribe would sway this man. "You're not going to hurt my family are you?" was the only thing he could think to ask as he resigned himself to his fate.

"No Barry, I'm not. I'm not really a bad guy, truth be told. I doubt that sounds realistic to you under the current circumstances but I don't really give a fuck. I've spent a lifetime trying to be good while others do what they want, and life always seems to bite me in the arse anyway. Yet scum roam the earth, polluting it with their spawn…the next generation of shite who will ruin good people's lives. If it was up to me I'd put you all down, since most people are cunts. It's just the way of it; humans are selfish creatures who try to kid themselves that they are more important than they really are. Personally, I think most people just go along with the status quo for an easy ride. Why rock the boat? It doesn't really matter anymore. When I'm done with you, I will take my own life and join my family.

Barry squirmed in his chair. He already knew there was no way to escape but it was clear that Alec was coming to the end of the proceedings and if he was ever going to get out of here, it would have to be now. With one final burst of strength he flexed against the cords that tied him to the chair and broke down sobbing with the realisation that this was it, he was going to die very soon and no one was coming to rescue him.

"Alec, please! If not for me then for my daughters!" Barry begged.

"Sorry, mate. I need you. Look around you. What's missing? Yeh, that's right. You guessed it. A Christmas tree! That's where you come in, my friend." As Alex finished speaking, he put the gag back into Barry's mouth and tied it tight behind his head. He had heard enough, had toyed with him enough—it was time to end it all.

Alec marched back into the kitchen and reappeared almost immediately, dragging a large cardboard box with 'Tree decorations' scribbled on the side, and left it sitting next to Barry. "It looks like you will need to step in as our Christmas tree, mate." Alec made his way over to the laptop and after a minute 'Rockin' Around the Christmas Tree' started to play from the speakers. Alec smiled as it drowned out the sound of Barry sobbing through his gag. As far as Alec could tell, at least he had stopped trying to beg for his miserable life. Alec leaned down into the box, grabbed a long red piece of tinsel and started to wrap it around Barry, working from his feet up. The tinsel still had little tabs of tape stuck to it from last year; there wasn't much glue left on it, but enough that it hung around him as it would a tree. He leaned back in and this time grabbed a long green piece and repeated the procedure. Alec stepped back and took a look at Barry. Sitting in the chair he was wider at the bottom with his knees sticking out and thinner at the top; Alec thought it looked pretty good if a little sparse. He grabbed one more piece, silver this time and again wrapped it around his new 'Christmas tree'. His wife had always liked baubles, and while he wasn't a fan, he believed you should keep the wife happy, so they'd always had them. For a split second Alec toyed with the idea of nailing them to his victim but he doubted Barry would last long enough. He grabbed a roll of tape that still lay in the box and started biting off little strips. When he had about twenty he started taping the baubles all over Barry, some seemed to have trouble sticking so Alec was a little over excessive with the tape. When he was done with the baubles, he reached into the box and grabbed a can of spray snow. "This is the part my kids used to love doing," he remarked to Barry as he began to cover him with the stuff. There was a little hitch in his voice as he said it. Once he had finished he disappeared into the kitchen again and came back with a box of Christmas lights. "Thought I'd forgotten, didn't you?" he asked, knowing there would be no answer. "Normally we use the same old lights, but who can be bothered untangling them all? It's not like I need to watch my money carefully now, anyway." Alec ripped the box open, tossed it aside and started to wrap them around Barry. The spray snow seemed to have gotten into Barry's eyes because it didn't look like he could see very well anymore. Alec was a little disappointed that Barry wouldn't see how good he looked. Alec walked over to the wall and plugged the lights in, then flipped the switch so they would flicker and change colour. He stood back admiring his work; he had done a good job, but it needed just one last touch. He went to the box again and retrieved the Christmas star that he had jammed down onto a tent spike so it would work. He stepped up and in front of Barry, raised it high above his head and slammed it down, double handed with all the force he could muster. The peg pierced Barry's skull and sank in, his body going into such spasms, Alec had to grab the chair to keep it from tipping over. Barry died quickly and Alec again stepped back to admire his work. His 'tree' looked much better with the star, and though it did hang to one side, the star had always been too heavy and caused the tops of their trees to hang sideways. Blood was running from the peg down Barry's face but as it was red, it didn't look too out of place with the decorations wrapped around him.

Alec stood in front of Barry for a few minutes, not really paying any attention to his creation, his mind just wandering through previous Christmases with his family. The sirens coming from somewhere not too far in the distance was what snapped Alec back to reality. With no more than an accepting nod, Alec went back into the kitchen and returned carrying his nail gun. He sat in the chair facing his new tree and pulled out a picture of Pauline, Sarah and Sammy that he had taken a few days before he lost them. He sat looking at it, nail gun hanging at his side. He could hear the sirens getting closer as a tear dripped onto the photo. "I'm sorry I couldn't save you," he whispered sadly. Alec raised the nail gun so that it was pointing upwards, then placed it under his chin and, clenching the picture tightly, his finger began to push against the trigger when he suddenly felt someone touch his shoulder. Whipping around quickly and finding no one there, he then heard his wife's voice saying, "No, Alec, not yet. There are other bad men to punish. Go. Go now before they get here. Your job isn't done yet."

"Pauline… baby," he responded tearfully, but she was gone and he knew it. Wasting no time, Alec was up and out of his chair, dropping the nail gun next to it. He went straight for the back door and left it wide open as he ran out into a bright Christmas morning. He couldn't get caught just yet. There *were* more bad men to punish. "Merry fuckin' Christmas!" he said to no one but himself as he disappeared out into the day, thinking that he wouldn't let his wife down this time.

The End

Christmas on the Streets

Every Christmas, I wander the streets of your town. I wander the streets of every city and town as it goes. You've seen me. You didn't notice me though. I used to be someone. I used to be important. I stand there with my hand out, begging for change. My clothes are dirty, my beard has food in it, and I sway on the spot. You can smell the cheap alcohol on my breath as you pass and you avert your eyes, knowing if you make eye contact, you will feel bad for me. It's easier to just keep walking. Why stop? You are busy, things to be getting on with. Money is tight, times are hard. You have gifts to buy for your loved ones. I used to love giving gifts myself but that was in a different life, my old life. I've been on the streets for a while. Few care. There are too many on the streets now.

I no longer wear the hat, I no longer have the red jacket and trousers, the black boots are gone. There are no jingle bells and no reindeer. There is only me, the magical old man. It was fun being Claus and it's fun being the Reaper. People live and people grow. Sometimes we change for the better and sometimes we change for the worse. Maybe it's all just down to perspective. A job is just that, a job. I try not to get too caught up in what I do. I don't let it define me. I'm only the Christmas Reaper. I only work one month a year, so I guess I can't complain. The uniform isn't as nice but jobs are hard to come by these days. If you see me looking in your window though, this may just be your last Christmas, or maybe you are just watching a show that I like and I'm on my break. Time is short for all though and it passes by quickly. I'll be seeing you sooner or later. Merrryyyyyyy Christmas!

The End

One Shift Too Many

One Thousand, seven hundred and forty years Santa had been doing his job. In the beginning he loved that he brought joy to children. After a thousand years he liked the fact that he only worked once a year. After fifteen hundred years he only liked that Mrs Claus didn't age. After seventeen hundred years, he hated the job completely. Forty years after that, he liked the way the blood splattered on the walls of the toy factory as he slaughtered the elves mercilessly. "Ho fucking ho!" he screamed as he danced between them, swinging a candy cane like scythe.

The Christmas Surprise

When Mary woke up on Christmas morning, she felt a little rough. She had gone for a few drinks after work with the girls and the few turned into many. She had no plans whatsoever for Christmas day though, so she wasn't too worried. Being single at Christmas suited Mary just fine. Less presents to buy. She didn't even care about spending the money. It was just trying to find things that people would appreciate. She always talked herself out of any ideas she came up with and it would go on and on. She had sent a few gifts out in the post a week ago and made up her mind that this year she would stay home and do exactly what she wanted. No trying to please anyone else, no eating something you are supposed to eat on the big day. It would simply be a day of indulgence, and anyway, a few more drinks would knock the minor hangover away.

As she came downstairs, she decided the drink would probably be the best way to kick off the day. A day alone was really the best treat she could give herself. She never got time alone. She was either working, working from home, socialising, or helping someone out with something. When she did get home and had free time, it was generally spent sleeping. She walked into the kitchen and went straight to the drink's cupboard. She pulled a bottle of violet gin out and walked over to the refrigerator. She removed a mostly full bottle of lemonade and sat them both on the worktop. Next, she collected a glass from the sideboard and poured herself a large one. Taking a sip, she let out a relaxed moan and began to make her way to the living room, grabbing a bag of Flaming Hot Monster Munch on her way out the door. She walked across the hall and was just entering the living room when there was a knock at the door. She threw her bag of chips on the sofa and placed the glass on the small table next to the couch. Puling her robe tighter around herself she made her way to the front door. *Who could possibly be calling on*

Christmas day, she thought. A little annoyed by the intrusion.

Mary pulled the door open and looked around. No one stood in the doorway. She stepped outside and searched for anyone rushing away. She stayed at the end of a fairly quiet street and had a large garden. There was no way that someone could have left so quickly. She was just about to step back inside when she noticed a gift at her feet. It was beautifully wrapped in expensive silver paper and had a gorgeous red bow on top. She lent down and picked it up. It was freezing so after another quick glance around, Mary went back inside and closed the door, locking it behind her. She went back into the living room and flopped down onto the sofa. She stared at the present while she lifted her gin. After taking a large swallow and placing the glass back down, Mary lifted the gift off her knee and turned it around slowly. There was no tag, and nothing written on the paper. *Who could it be from?* After some careful thought, she decided to tear it open. The suspense was too much, and she wasn't the type to save wrapping paper, lovely or not. As the paper came away, she noticed the box was nothing fancy. No branding or anything, just plain brown. Once the paper was gone, she lifted the lid off it and instantly let out a laugh when she seen that someone had sent her, a rather large dildo, or possibly vibrator but whatever it was, it was cock shaped. It did have white and red stripes wrapping round it like a candy cane, but it was the wrong shape.

"Must have been one of those assholes from work." Mary said out loud.

She had never gone in for the secret Santa. Maybe someone had decided to send her a joke gift anyway. She sat the box on the floor to the side of the sofa, kicked her legs up and lifted her drink. She took another sip and switched the TV on, went straight to Netflix and put National Lampoons Christmas Vacation on. She had decided her play list over a week ago. Christmas Vacation, Elf, Klaus, A Bad Mums Christmas and then Krampus. It would take up most of the day and she loved them all.

As the movie began to play, she realised she had finished her drink. Luckily, it had been the exact curer she had needed.

"I think I deserve another." She said to the little Snowman ornament that sat on her fireplace. She got up to go get another drink and imagined if the little snowman had answered her back. She got a shiver down her spine and had a nervous chuckle. The snowman said nothing, she got her drink and made her way back to the sofa. As she watched Chevy Chase cause carnage everywhere he went, she chuckled away to herself.

She ate the Monster Munch, sipping at her gin to cool down the nip they gave her mouth. She took the second drink a little slower, feeling much more relaxed than she did with the first one.

As the movie came to an end, she found herself glancing at the gift. She was all alone and had nothing to do. Maybe she should give it a whirl. She finished off her drink and lifted it onto her lap. It was bigger than she would have bought herself but that didn't mean it wouldn't be fun. Maybe just a little buzz on her button would be enough. She looked around it and couldn't see anywhere to put batteries but there were buttons on it. She clicked the first button and it buzzed to life. She tried the second and it started playing Jingle Bells. Thinking this would be off putting, she turned it back off. The third button didn't seem to do anything. She lay back on the sofa, parted her robe and put it to her clit through her panties. It was strong enough that she wouldn't need to remove them, for now at least. It was definitely an expensive piece of kit. She had owned many vibrators through the years but had never owned one that didn't need batteries and the vibrations were strong on the lowest setting. She found herself pulling her panties to the side and replacing the toy to her now throbbing clit. It didn't take long at all before she was digging her heels into the sofa and screaming obscenities to no one in particular. She collapsed backwards and began to laugh.

"Merry Fucking Christmas indeed." She said lazily eyeing the toy that now lay soaked on her thigh.

After lying in a bit of a daze for ten minutes or so, Mary got up and made her way to the kitchen. It was time she had another drink and maybe time to watch another movie and relax. She poured the drink and got back to the sofa, flicked on Elf. What she didn't notice, thanks to there being no mirrors downstairs, was that her ears had grown and had an elf like point to them now. She didn't feel them change and had no idea that her appearance was altered. What was more alarming though was there was now a little peak at the top of her head. Almost unnoticeable but it was there none the less.

As Elf played through and Mary slowly sipped away at her drink, her mind wandered. She thought about previous Christmases, putting up old trees, her parents, playing in the snow as a kid, sledding and all sorts of other things she hadn't thought about for years. Christmas now was just a chance for a few days off. She had lost the spirit, but it was playing on her mind.

The movie ended and Mary's glass was empty once again. She felt a nice glow and decided it might be time to have another go on the candy cane type vibrator. She quickly ripped her knickers down her legs as the anticipation overtook her. She had never been so excited about using a toy. She tossed her panties across the room and grabbed the toy from its box, she hit the on button and started to put it on her pussy. She wasn't quite sure why but this time she kept thinking that it would be better with the music playing so she hit the other button and it began playing Jingle Bells. She pressed it back to her clit and it wasn't long before she was squirting all over the couch. Normally she would put a towel down if she was going to make a mess but she had never squirted before without penetrating herself. It took her a while to catch her breath. Likely because she didn't even realise she was holding it at first and then she began panting. She tried to get off the sofa and her legs buckled. It took her a few minutes before she was fit to stand up and walk. She went to the kitchen, poured herself another drink and returned to the soaked sofa. Plonking herself down she lay back and took a sip of her gin before placing it on the floor. She started up another movie, choosing Klaus this time. She was enjoying the start of the movie, but something was tugging at her brain to have another go on the toy. She lifted her drink and took a large gulp, telling herself that she needed to calm down. As Klaus played on, her attention waned. She kept glimpsing at the candy cane coloured plastic and telling herself one more go wouldn't hurt. What Mary hadn't yet realised was that her ears had gown a little larger again. The peak of her head was also a little taller. Not only that, but had she not been wearing extra thick wool socks, she would have seen that her feet were getting hairy. Her nose was taking on an orange tinge, but her nose was so tiny, she couldn't even see it on her own face.

Running out of patience and no longer paying any attention to the movie, Mary took another drink of the gin, flung the glass on the floor, the remaining contents going everywhere and snatched the toy from the box. It was still wet from her last exploits and this time she wasted no time in sticking it straight in. She was no longer satisfied with external stimulation. She would ride the toy like a Blackpool donkey. She hit buttons one and two and rode it as she hummed Jingle Bells and tried the third button again but nothing. She knelt on the sofa, bent over, arms on the back of it and stuffed the toy in like she was stuffing a turkey. She gave herself a right good battering with it until the point where she could barely keep a hold on it. Her toy, her hand and the couch were a mess. Once again, she collapsed on the sofa and dropped the toy into the box. She lay panting for a good twenty minutes. This time when she went to the kitchen for a drink, she just grabbed the bottle and swigged straight from it as she flopped back onto the sofa.

She pressed play for A Bad Mum's Christmas to come on, but she wasn't really sure why anymore. Sitting back, robe spread, legs lying open, Mary swigged from the bottle of Gin. She didn't feel drunk or even tipsy, she felt like her mind was somewhere else completely. As Mary began to reminisce about all the best bits of previous Christmases, the colours in the room began to distort. Her vision was okay, but everything looked to be tinged slightly red, green, white or gold. If she could have seen her eyes, she would have realised this might be because of the physical change. Her eyes were now completely black. No white at all, just all pupil. The point in her head was at least four inches tall now and her nose had grown at least two inches. It was even brighter orange and had several bumps along it like a carrot. Her ears had grown another inch and a thin layer of white hair covered a good part of her body. Although Mary was still able to move, her self-awareness was slipping away. She no longer paid any attention to the TV. The movie had been put on autopilot. She sipped at the bottle but only because it was in her hand. Her coal black eyes stared at the candy cane in the box. Her mouth watered, saliva running down her exposed chest. She didn't notice. Her pussy pulsed, her gammon curtains twitched. Her clit was throbbin' like a robin. Every fibre of her being told her to slam the toy into her meat pocket and show it who was boss. And, seconds later, that's exactly what she did. This time she knelt on the floor and lay her chest on the sofa for balance. She stuffed the toy straight inside. It fit perfectly. It was as if it was seeking out parts of her pussy that had never been touched. She had the vibrations turned up full and the toy was belting out Jingle Bells when she decided to give the third button a try again. This time, something happened. She heard something inside the toy whirring into action. She continued to punish herself with hard strokes as she jingled her way to another tsunami of an orgasm when the toy clicked. It began to elongate itself and she could feel it plunging deeper into her love tunnel. She stopped rattling herself and just held still. The toy seemed to be growing in diameter too. As she felt herself being filled something else clicked and then she felt it. Letting lose a scream that could have been heard three towns away. Hundreds of tiny metal spikes shot from the vibrator and pierced the inside of her wizard's sleeve. They cut deep and hooked in so that no matter how Mary tried to remove the toy, it was stuck deep. She began to panic but then she felt her mind start to wander. Jingle bells began to play again, and it was so soothing. Turning over, she lay back on the sofa but left the bottom half of her body hanging off. Blood dripped down the inside of her thighs and pooled on the carpet. She lazily lifted the bottle of gin and took a few gulps as her mind became hazy. The blades from the toy cut deeper into Mary and connected to several internal organs, joints, bones and muscles. Mary's nose grew longer and became even more orange. Her black eyes took on a bulbous quality. Her ears grew further and were now larger than her head. Her fur grew thicker and covered almost all her skin. Sharp claws ruptured her feet and burst threw her socks and the candy cane vibe hung three inches out of her minge, the rest still inside her.

Mary lay unmoving until midnight struck. As Christmas passed by, Mary was born again, as something new, as something terrifying. She wasn't the only one. Hundreds of thousands of anonymous gifts were received on Christmas day. Most were opened. Almost every one was used. A Christmas army of evil was formed, and Krampus was coming. Not for Christmas but for the other three hundred and sixty-four days of the year. He had more time than Santa Claus and now he had more Christmas Clunge Monsters than Santa had elves. The war was on.

The End

Down the Bizarro Watering Hole

On the last work day of the year, the minutes seemed to pass by slower than any other day. Tiffany could never understand why they had to work on Christmas Eve anyway. No one did anything. The entire morning was spent killing time. They always got a half day though there was no set time to leave. The entire staff had to sit around waiting on an email coming from the owner, telling them they could all go home. It could be anytime between twelve- thirty and two- thirty. Most of the staff took turns sneaking out to buy last minute Christmas gifts. Since Tiffany already had in what she needed she would spend the entire day surfing the net. The Christmas party had been the night before and she was still hungover—another reason that it made no sense to have anyone in on the twenty fourth. It was just all-round stupid.

At ten past two the email arrived. By this point Tiffany was at a boiling point. She had popped out at lunch time and had two double vodka cokes to take the edge off but returning to work to sit and wait on a stupid email had put her in a foul mood. She had no plans for Christmas Day as her family all lived across the sea and her presents had been posted already, so she had nothing in particular to do, which suited her fine. When the email popped into her inbox, she pushed the power button on her PC and shouted, "Have a good Christmas everyone!" as she walked out the door. She could not be bothered with all the kisses and cuddles and fake platitudes. While there was no one in the office that she particularly disliked, there was also no one she particularly liked either. It was a job. She was there to make money to pay her bills and that was all.

Tiffany's friends were all spending Christmas Day with their families and none of them planned to get drunk on Christmas Eve. They all wanted to be fresh for the day and enjoy Christmas dinner, which she could understand. A few of them had invited her to join them at their family dinners and while she knew the offers were genuine, she didn't want to be the hanger-on at another family's special day. She was quite content to spend time alone, never being one to feel sad about things like that. Christmas was a special day when you were with the ones you loved, but when you were on your own, it was just another day. There was no sadness attached. It was just a fact.

As Tiffany stepped out of the elevator and made her way out of the building, she decided that another few drinks would bring her back to the land of the living, then she would head home and find a few good movies to watch while having a last few drinks in her apartment. She planned to have a very long lie in in the morning. That would be her Christmas gift to herself.

Walking along the street she decided to head towards her apartment and find a bar close to home, so she could get back quickly and get into her jammies. She had bought new PJs for the night, a tradition that she had never let go of, even though she was all alone. They had little cartoon reindeer on them that wore Santa hats. She had changed her bed covers before going to the Christmas party the day before and had slept on the sofa last night for the few hours' sleep she got, so the bed would be fresh and inviting when she got in. She was looking forward to chilling out and was running through movies she may watch in her mind when she noticed a new bar across the street. The red neon sign read 'Bizarro,' and she thought it seemed like a strange name for a bar but decided it would do for a quick few drinks and crossed the road.

Inside, the bar was almost empty. She felt quite happy with that, feeling no need for Christmas revellers bothering her and making small talk. She perched herself on a bar stool with some difficulty. Pencil skirts weren't designed for stepping up onto high chairs, but she managed, albeit in a slightly unladylike fashion. She looked around while she waited on the currently non-existent bartender. There were a few people sitting at the back of the bar, but it was relatively dark. They seemed to be having a quiet conversation and paid her no attention.

"Help you?" came a question from across the bar.

"Give me a shot of anything."

Tiffany had decided a few shots would give her a quick kick and remove the hangover that was coming back, and then she would have a few of her favourite whiskys and get herself home. She didn't want it to turn into a late one, but shots were quick and then she would sip her whisky for a nice glow. Getting home and slipping into her warm bed to watch a movie would be much nicer if she was a little tipsy compared to lying there hungover.

"Bizarro?"

"Excuse me!"

"The shot. Would you like a Bizarro?"

"Uh, yeah. I'll give it a go."

She slipped a ten-pound note across the bar and the bar man returned, gave her the drink and lifted the money. She knocked it back straight away. It tasted like sherbet dip but had a burn to it too. She could feel it reaching her stomach. Almost immediately she could feel a warmth rise through her and it felt as if she was tipsy already. She shook her head and rubbed her eyes.

"I definitely had too much to drink last night," she muttered to herself.

When Tiffany opened her eyes, the bar was no longer in front of her.

"What the fuck?"

"We will have none of that language here young lady," came a voice from behind her.

She spun around. She now faced an enormous chair next to a roaring fire where sat what could only be described as a black panther in a Santa suit. Even more strange was the fact that it was sitting upright in the chair like a human would. It genuinely looked like it was smiling at her.

"Did you just... Did you just talk?"

"Well, of course I did. Do you see anyone else here?"

"No, but, you're a panther."

"A what?" it responded.

"A panther."

"I am Santa Claus. Nothing more. Nothing less."

"Wait! Santa is a fat jolly old guy with a beard."

"Is he?"

It was definitely smiling.

"Yeh, he fucking is. What do you mean is he? Have you been living in a cave?"

"I've lived in many places, my child."

Tiffany could feel herself getting pissed off.

"What's going on? Where am I?"

"You are exactly where you are supposed to be, child," the panther replied.

"Will you stop calling me 'child'?"

Tiffany racked her brain for what could possibly be happening and wondered if the bartender slipped something into her drink. She shook her head, rubbed her eyes again and took a deep breath. Upon opening her eyes, she was still facing the black panther in the Santa suit.

"Okay. I'll play along. Why am I here?" Tiffany asked, trying to calm herself down.

"Only you can answer that question, child."

"I fucking told y…" Tiffany caught herself and took another deep breath. "Okay… How do I get out of here?"

"Well, why do you think you are here?"

After another few deep breaths and a mental lecture to not lose her cool, realising it wasn't getting her anywhere, Tiffany decided to try and talk it out. If it was anything like a bad dream or trip, the best she could do would be to try and keep it as happy as possible and avoid any bad outcomes.

"I'm guessing I have had one too many. Either that or I have been sucked into a low budget reimagining of Scrooge. Either way, I'm ready to go home to my bed, so if we could move it along, that would be just dandy."

"Tell me your thoughts on Christmas, my child," the irritating panther said. It had a low, smooth voice that Tiffany felt she could almost fall asleep to if she was in a better frame of mind.

"Well, I'm guessing it's to help me realise some life-changing affirmation, but I'm pretty happy with how my life is going, so, as I said, can we move things along?"

"If you are happy, you wouldn't be here. What are your Christmas plans, child?"

"My plan is to get home and wrap myself up in a nice warm bed. I'll spend all night watching cheesy Christmas movies if you will just get me out of here. Good enough for you?"

"Is it good enough for you?" came the response.

"Holy fuck, are you the Riddler or a fake Santa? Come on, how do I get home?"

"Just ask, child."

"Can I go home, fake Santa panther?"

The Santa panther smiled just as Tiffany blinked. As her eyes opened back up, she found herself sitting in a bar with an empty shot glass in front of her.

"No fucking way!" she exclaimed

Tiffany knew there was no way her drink could have been spiked. Tripping rarely came and went as quickly. She checked her watch and only a minute had passed. She spun back around towards the bar, which had returned to its normal place and there was another shot in front of her. She knew she hadn't ordered another, but she wasn't ready to go home yet and the side of her that often got her into trouble told her to have it and see how the night played out. The other part was telling her to get straight home to bed where she would be safe, but she had never been great at taking advice from that side. She lifted the shot and quickly knocked it back. She got the same warm feeling, but this time kept her eyes open.

Deciding she would keep an eye on the bar. Eventually, the need to blink was too strong. Her eye lids closed then opened and once again the bar was gone. She was less shocked this time. She spun in her chair expecting to see the Santa panther, but this time in front of her was her mum and dad's living room.

"What the actual fuck?" she said aloud.

The living room was exactly as she remembered it. Her mother and father sat in their arm chairs at either side of a roaring fire. They both wore a different pair of Christmas pyjamas. It was Tiffany's mother who had started the tradition of new Christmas pyjamas and socks every year. She would buy them all a pair. It was the only day of the year that her father wore pyjamas, but he did it gladly to keep her mother happy. Tiffany knew he was a big softy when it came to Christmas too.

"What do you think Tiffany is up to tonight?" her mother said.

"Oh, I'm sure she will be out partying with her friends. It's a shame when they get too old to come home," her father replied, looking into some far-off place.

"I really miss her, honey."

"Me too, dear, me too. She's an adult now, though. We need to let her live her life."

Tiffany could hear the sadness in both of their voices. She realised she was crying as tears ran down each cheek.

"Maybe when her life quietens down a little, she will come home and visit more," her mother said, sounding wishful.

"I hope so, I really do."

Tiffany wanted to run over and give them both the biggest hug and tell them that she was sorry, that she loved them and had no idea they missed her so much. She somehow knew that this time she wouldn't be able to talk to the apparition. It was like watching a video. She wasn't sure how she knew, but she knew she was right. More tears filled her eyes and she struggled to see. She brought both hands up to her eyes and rubbed them, trying to clear the tears away. As her eyes cleared, she was back in the bar and facing a plain black wall. She spun quickly round in her chair to the bar, and yet again, there was another shot. Wasting no time, she slammed it back. She wanted to know if there was more to see. This time she closed her eyes straight away and began spinning round as she began to open them again.

This time, things were different. Tiffany was standing outside her parent's house. The strange thing was that her parents lived in the middle of a housing estate but the house in front of her stood on its own. It was unmistakably her parent's home, though. She could never forget the place she grew up. There was no time for contemplating why she was here or wondering if it was going to be one of those sad moments from the movies that made her reflect on everything. Her parent's house was under attack. There were green goblin-looking animals everywhere. They wore badly fitting elf costumes. Most had humped backs with ridged spines that had torn through the material in some places. They ran around chaotically, going between standing upright and running on all fours. Some were throwing stones or bricks at the windows. Some of them were trying to beat the front door down and others were climbing up onto the roof.

Tiffany shook her head, trying to clear her thoughts. She looked down at the weight in her right hand to see she was holding a pump action shotgun. Strapped to her two thighs were two Dessert Eagle .50's— not that she knew what that was. Just that she had a gun strapped to either leg. She had never held a real gun in her life, nevertheless she felt like she knew how to use them. Her entire body was clad in black clothes, making her look like an assassin from a Hollywood movie.

When Tiffany began to walk towards the house she moved with purpose. Whether this was a dream, hallucination, or reality, she did not know. In any case, no little green monster was going to hurt her parents. She brought the shotgun up and pointed it at the first elf that noticed her and started running at her. She kept her calm and waited until it was close and pulled the trigger. The elf exploded into pieces and left a huge red blood- splatter pattern where it had been standing. Only its two legs remained. She pumped another shell into the shotgun and continued moving forward. By the time she got to the house, the shotgun was empty. She watched another elf run towards her, flipped the gun upside down and used it to deliver a home run swing at the elf's head. She absolutely obliterated the creature's head and dropped the empty shotgun where she stood. She had known she could have pulled a gun but something inside her wanted to smash the elf's head open.

Once again, she moved closer to the house. The creatures were everywhere. She drew the Desert Eagle .50 and started putting rounds into each of the mutated elves. She felt good as she did it. She watched them drop onto their front sides or back sides and squirm around. She knew they were suffering and that's what she wanted. None of them got a mercy shot to end their lives. They had picked the wrong house.

When all the elves in front of the house were dead, she started shooting the ones that had made it to the roof. She enjoyed watching them roll off and smash into the ground. Once she had cleared the roof, she walked around the perimeter. There were none at the back or sides of the house, but a few windows had been smashed in and she wasn't sure if any had got down the chimney. Knowing that the front door may be locked, she climbed in through one of the broken windows. No sooner had her feet touched the carpet than she heard a scream from upstairs. She knew it was her mother's voice.

"Not a fucking chance. Little green fucks," Tiffany growled, already moving through the house.

There were none downstairs. As she began to ascend the stairs, they started throwing things down at her. It did not slow her down. They retreated into her parents' room where she knew they would have found her mother. Tiffany kicked the door so hard it nearly came off the hinges. As she entered, she had both guns drawn. There were at least fifteen of the ugly little things in there. Five of them were holding her mother. She wondered if the things had murdered elves and stolen their clothing or if this was what they looked like and this bunch had just gone bad. Either way, they were dead. She shot two in the chest and brought the guns round to shoot another two between the eyes. She looked back at her mother each time the triggers were pulled. She noticed that her mother kept looking into the corner. Risking a quick look, Tiffany saw two legs sticking out from the bottom of the bed. She knew instantly that they were her father's and that he was dead. Even though Tiffany wasn't sure if any of this was real, her eyes filled with tears. She didn't know when she got back to reality if her father would be dead or alive. She pointed the guns at two of the monsters that held her mother and just as she was squeezing the trigger, one of them stabbed her mother in the chest.

"Noooooo!" Tiffany screamed.

She began unloading her guns into anything in the room that was green. In a matter of seconds, nothing moved apart from her mother slumping to the floor. She ran over to her and put her hands behind her head. As she pulled her mother's head up to look at her, the light went from her eyes. Tiffany was just about to scream again when her eyesight disappeared. Everything went black and then she was back in the bar, arms resting on the bar, hands over her eyes and bawling her eyes out.

"You okay little lady?" the barman asked from the other side of the bar, making his way over.

Tiffany was up and out of the bar in seconds. The street looked exactly as it had when she entered, but everything else had changed. She no longer wanted to go back to her apartment. New jammies and Christmas movies weren't going to cut it. She needed her mom. Before Tiffany knew what she was doing, she was in a cab and heading to the airport. She had no idea where the new bar had come from or what was in those shots she had. She had never experienced anything similar before and hoped she never would again, but on this one occasion she was glad she had gone in. She wanted to see her parents. She couldn't remember why she always put it off. She regretted all the time she had missed with them. Maybe she was just trying to prove her independence and had taken it too far. Maybe it was more than that, but she knew one thing. She would never miss a Christmas with her parents ever again.

A few hours later…

Tiffany sat on the plane waiting for take-off. She had never been as excited to go home. She had thought about calling her parents from the airport to tell them she was coming but had decided to make it a surprise. Her body buzzed with excitement. She knew her mom would have enough food in for an extra person, she knew they would be delighted to see her even though they would be sleeping when she arrived. She no longer had a key, so she would have to wake them up. She also knew her mom would have bought her a new pair of Christmas jammies, just in case she appeared. She really did have the best parents. She wondered if after Christmas it might be time to look for a new job, closer to home.

The End

Printed in Great Britain
by Amazon